THE MISSING PLAYBOOK

Don't miss any of the cases in the Hardy Boys Clue Book series!

HARDY BOYS

→Clue Book←

#2

THE MISSING PLAYBOOK

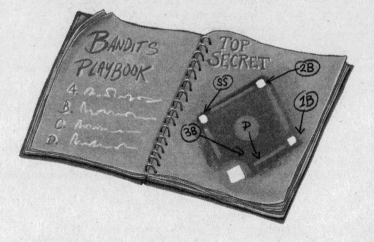

BY FRANKLIN W. DIXON ⟻ ILLUSTRATED BY MATT DAVID

ALADDIN

NEW YORK   LONDON   TORONTO   SYDNEY   NEW DELHI

This book is a work of fiction. Any references to historical events, real people,
or real places are used fictitiously. Other names, characters, places, and events are
products of the author's imagination, and any resemblance to actual events or
places or persons, living or dead, is entirely coincidental.

ALADDIN

An imprint of Simon & Schuster Children's Publishing Division
1230 Avenue of the Americas, New York, NY 10020
This Aladdin paperback edition April 2016
Text copyright © 2016 by Simon & Schuster, Inc.
Illustrations copyright © 2016 by Matt David
Also available in an Aladdin hardcover edition.
All rights reserved, including the right of reproduction in whole or in part in any form.
ALADDIN is a trademark of Simon & Schuster, Inc., and related logo is
a registered trademark of Simon & Schuster, Inc.
THE HARDY BOYS and colophons are registered trademarks of Simon & Schuster, Inc.
HARDY BOYS CLUE BOOK and colophons are trademarks of Simon & Schuster, Inc.
For information about special discounts for bulk purchases, please contact
Simon & Schuster Special Sales at 1-866-506-1949 or business@simonandschuster.com.
The Simon & Schuster Speakers Bureau can bring authors to your live event.
For more information or to book an event contact the Simon & Schuster Speakers Bureau
at 1-866-248-3049 or visit our website at www.simonspeakers.com.
Book designed by Karina Granda
The text of this book was set in Adobe Garamond Pro.
Manufactured in the United States of America 0419 OFF
4 6 8 10 9 7 5
Library of Congress Control Number 2015938960
ISBN 978-1-4814-5178-9 (hc)
ISBN 978-1-4814-5177-2 (pbk)
ISBN 978-1-4814-5179-6 (eBook)

CONTENTS

THE MISSING PLAYBOOK

BASEBALL BARBECUE

As soon as his father pulled up to Cissy "Speedy" Zermeño's house, Joe Hardy threw open the car door and ran up to the house. Frank smiled and rolled his eyes at his eight-year-old younger brother. On the inside, though, Frank was just as excited as Joe was about the party at Speedy's. The annual Bandit Barbecue dinner meant the beginning of baseball season, his favorite time of year.

Frank grabbed the plate of brownies his mother

had made, and his parents followed him up the walkway to the Zermeños' front door. Joe had already disappeared somewhere inside, and Speedy was waiting at the door to greet them. Speedy's real name was Cissy, but she got her nickname from how quickly she did everything, from the speed of her legendary fastball to how quickly she talked.

"Hi-Mr.-and-Mrs.-Hardy-hey-Frank-come-on-in!" she said. *"I'm-so-excited-you're-here-wow-those-brownies-look-delicious!"*

"Hi, Speedy," Frank said. "How's the wrist?"

"Great!" Speedy held up her right hand. The last time Frank had seen her in school on Friday, she'd been wearing a brace. But now it was gone. *"The-doctor-said-the-sprain—"*

"Whoa, whoa!" Frank interrupted. "Slow down!"

Speedy laughed and took a deep breath before she spoke again, more slowly this time. "The doctor said my sprain is almost completely healed. He says I'll be able to pitch in our first game next week!"

"That's awesome!" Frank exclaimed. Speedy, along with the rest of the team, had been worried when she'd hurt her wrist in gym class a couple of weeks ago. She was their star pitcher, and without her, they didn't stand a chance against their rivals the Jupiters.

"*Oh-I-know!* I can't wait to pitch the first game!" Speedy said.

Frank and Mr. and Mrs. Hardy followed Speedy outside to the backyard, where the barbecue was in full swing. Mr. and Mrs. Hardy stopped to talk to the other parents, while Frank and Speedy went looking for Joe. They found him at the backyard swing set with the Mortons. Frank and Joe's best friend, Chet, was taking turns pushing his two younger sisters—Iola, who played for the Bandits, and Mimi, who went everywhere Iola did—on the swings. A camera was hanging from a strap around Chet's neck.

"Hi, Chet," Frank said. He nodded at the camera. "You taking pictures of the party?"

"Yup!" Chet said. He gave Iola a push and then grabbed his camera, holding it up for Frank to see. "There are so many cool things you can do with this camera!" He began to explain to Frank how all the different buttons worked.

"Chet!" Mimi wailed. Her swing had come to a stop because Chet, distracted by his camera, had forgotten to push her. When Chet had a new hobby, he forgot about everything else.

"Oh, sorry," he said. He gave her a big push that sent her flying up into the air.

"What's that on your back, Mimi?" Joe asked.

"My new backpack!" Mimi squealed, kicking her feet to keep the swing going. "Isn't it cool? It's got butterflies on it!"

"She's starting preschool in the fall," Iola explained. "She's barely taken that backpack off since Mom bought it for her."

"Because it's *cool*!" Mimi said.

"Well, I'm starved," Iola said, hopping off her swing. "Who wants to get a hamburger?"

Everyone else said they were hungry too, except for Chet.

"But I'll come with you guys," he said. "I want to take some pictures of the food. Coach Quinn said I could be the team's official photographer."

They all got into the line next to the grill. Speedy's dad was hard at work cooking up hamburgers and hot dogs, moving almost as fast as Speedy did. Standing in front of them in line was Tommy Dawson, who was an outfielder and relief pitcher for the Bandits, and Ezra Moore, who was new to the team.

"It's so unfair," Tommy complained to Ezra, loud enough that Frank could hear him. "I thought I was finally going to get to pitch."

"Sorry, dude," Ezra said, "but Speedy's the starting pitcher. You knew Coach Quinn was going to let her pitch as soon as her wrist was healed."

"She shouldn't be the starter anyway," Tommy said. "I'm ten

times better than she is. Coach Quinn's just got it in for me. I'm not going to let Coach get away with this."

"Tommy, calm down," Ezra said.

"No way. Forget this stupid team!" Tommy snapped. He stalked off, ignoring Ezra's attempts to stop him.

Ezra noticed Frank listening in on their conversation.

"He'll cool off," he said. "He's just disappointed."

Frank nodded. He was just glad Speedy hadn't heard what Tommy was saying.

The kids loaded up their plates with food and sat in the grass with some of the other Bandits to eat. When they were done, someone found a baseball and they started a game of catch. All the younger brothers and sisters of the Bandits players were sitting around Mimi, whose backpack was jammed full of coloring books, stuffed animals, and other toys that she was handing out. They played while the older kids tossed the ball and the parents watched, chatting as they sipped their cups of punch.

Soon it began to grow dark, and the party moved

inside. The parents gathered in the kitchen, while the little kids sat in front of the television in the living room to watch a movie. Mimi was among them, her empty backpack slung over her shoulders. While they watched the movie, most of the kids played with one of the toys or coloring books that Mimi had given them.

Meanwhile, Coach Quinn gathered all the Bandits together for a team meeting.

"Thanks for coming, everyone," she said when the team was sitting before her. "It's going to be the start of an awesome season, right?"

"Right!" they all chorused. Joe's voice was the loudest of all, Frank noticed. Coach Quinn's eyes twinkled. "That's what I thought. Now, let me show you our new secret weapon."

Chapter 2.

PRANK NIGHT

Coach Quinn pulled a bright-red notebook from her bag. It had PLAYBOOK printed across it in bold black letters. Chet's camera flashed as he took a picture.

"This is our new playbook," she explained. "I've been coming up with new training methods and batting lineups that are going to make us the best team we can be. We're going to work hard and play even harder, and then what's going to happen?"

"We're going to *win*!" Joe shouted, and the rest of the team cheered.

"And what else?" Coach Quinn asked.

"Have fun!" everyone yelled.

Coach Quinn laughed. "That's right! Now have a good time tonight, because the hard work starts tomorrow!"

The meeting over, the team members went back to the party. Frank asked Coach Quinn if he could look at the playbook, and she handed it to him. He flipped through it slowly. One section showed new drills that would help them become faster, stronger, and pitch the ball even better. Another section had a dozen different batting orders, one for any situation they might face. Frank's eyes widened as he took it all in. He could almost feel the championship trophy in his hands.

Joe tapped on his shoulder,

interrupting his fantasy of scoring the game-winning run at the championships.

"Frank, come on," he said. "We're playing Pin the Hat on the Ballplayer in the dining room."

Frank put the playbook down on the coffee table and headed after his brother. On his way, he nearly tripped over Mimi, who was sprawled on the floor, scribbling in a coloring book.

In the dining room, Speedy's mom was leading the game. She had tied a blindfold around Ezra Moore's eyes, and he was trying to stick a paper ball cap with tape on the back to the large poster of a baseball player tacked to the wall. After feeling around for a while, Ezra stuck the cap near the ballplayer's elbow. Everyone laughed and clapped when he took off the blindfold, stomped his foot, and said, "Darn it!"

Frank was watching Mrs. Zermeño put the blindfold on Iola as Chet snapped pictures, when Joe tapped his shoulder again.

"Hey, do you hear that?" Joe asked.

"Hear what?" Frank replied.

"It sounds like there's someone outside the window!"

Frank tried to listen, but he couldn't hear anything over the music, the laughter of the kids, and the chatter of the parents in the next room. He moved closer to the window with Joe and looked out over the Zermeños' side yard. It was dark, so there wasn't much to see, and he didn't hear anything.

Frank shook his head. "I think you're hearing things, little brother."

But then he saw movement in the yard from the corner of his eye. It looked like someone running, but they disappeared from view too quickly for him to get a good look.

"Wait, I think you're right," Frank said. "I think someone *is* out there."

"Told ya!" Joe said.

"Come on," Frank said. "Let's go look out the front windows."

"Hey, where are you guys going?" Chet asked as they headed to the living room.

"We think there's someone outside," Joe said. "We're going to go check."

Speedy overheard them. "I'm coming too!"

The kids made their way to the windows at the front of the house. Chet had his camera pressed to his eye to take a picture and ended up stepping on the stuffed animal Tommy Dawson's little sister was playing with.

"You hurt Snuggles!" the girl shrieked.

"Sorry!" Chet said.

Frank crouched in front of one of the big windows next to the front door of the house, nothing but his eyes peeking over the windowsill. Joe stood next to him, peering around the edge of the curtains. Chet and Speedy took the window on the other side of the door.

"I can't see anything," Chet said. "It's too dark outside."

By now, the rest of the team had noticed them leaving the dining room and had gathered around them.

"What's going on?" Iola asked.

"We heard something weird outside," Joe replied.

"Speedy, do you have any lights out there?" Frank asked.

She nodded. "There's a porch light."

"Can you turn it on?" Frank said.

"You bet!" Speedy moved to a light switch on the wall near the door. "Count of three?"

Frank nodded.

"One . . . two . . ." Speedy flipped the switch. *"Three!"*

Outside on the Zermeños' lawn, three kids, all dressed in dark clothes, froze. Around them, the trees were covered in toilet paper, which hung from the branches like garlands and swayed gently in the breeze. The grass was covered in red and blue Silly String, which spelled out BANDITS STINK!

After a moment of stunned silence—the Bandits staring at the mess in the yard and the pranksters staring at them—everything exploded into action. The kids outside started to run, dropping their armfuls of extra toilet paper and Silly String bottles, and the Bandits poured out of the house after them.

BANDITS VS. JUPITERS

"Stop them!" Frank yelled as the trio scattered in different directions. The Bandits took off after them. Frank and Joe ran toward Speedy's neighbors to the left, where the biggest of the pranksters had headed. Frank heard a cheer somewhere behind him as other members of the team caught one of the fleeing kids.

In the dark, Frank could just barely make out the outline of the person he was chasing. The kid ran around the side of the neighbor's house, and by the time Frank and Joe got there, he'd disappeared.

"Where did he go?" Joe said. "It's so dark out here."

"Shh," Frank whispered. "Let's just listen for a second."

The prankster couldn't have outrun them so fast. Frank was sure he was hiding somewhere among the bushes and trees in the yard. The two boys were silent for a moment, ears straining to pick up any sounds of movement, but they didn't hear anything.

Suddenly Frank had an idea.

"I guess we lost him," Frank said, loudly enough that his voice would carry across the yard. "Better just give up."

"What!" Joe squawked. "We can't just let him get away with—"

Frank nudged his brother and gave him a wink.

"There's no point, Joe," Frank said loudly. "Let's just go back."

Joe smiled as he understood his brother's plan. "Okay, you're right. Let's go."

The two boys walked away, pretending like they were headed back to Speedy's. But instead they hid around the corner of the neighbor's house. Frank held a finger to his lips, and Joe nodded. Now all they had to do was wait.

One minute passed, then two, and nothing happened. Frank began to think the prankster had actually gotten away. But then, just when he was about to give up, Frank heard the rustle of leaves as the other kid crept out of his hiding place behind a row of bushes.

"Go!" Frank cried.

He and Joe ran around the corner of the house. The prankster saw them and tried to get away, but Frank and Joe were too close. They caught the other kid, and all three of them went tumbling to the ground.

"We got 'im!" Joe exclaimed.

Frank looked into the prankster's face, which he could see for the first time.

"Conor Hound," he said. He should have known. Conor—a star player for the Bandits' rivals the

Jupiters—was the only boy he knew who was this big.

Coach Quinn came running around the corner, followed by a group of parents. "What's going on here?"

"We caught him, Coach Quinn!" Joe said. "This is one of the kids who was toilet-papering Speedy's house."

"You'd better come with me, Conor," the coach said. "Let him go, boys."

Frank, Joe, and Conor, who was hanging his head, followed Coach Quinn and the parents back to Speedy's house. Two other members of the Jupiters were already seated on the couch in the living room, their arms crossed over their chests. Conor sat down beside them with a scowl. Chet and Iola gave Frank and Joe high fives for catching him.

"I'm very disappointed by this unsportsmanlike behavior, gentlemen," Coach Quinn was saying to the Jupiters. "I'm going to have to call your parents."

"What a mess," Speedy said glumly, looking out the window at the toilet paper hanging from the trees.

"We'll help you clean it up," Iola promised.

"Yeah," Frank added. "Of course we will. Come on, everybody!"

"I think *they* should clean it up," Joe said, pointing at the boys on the couch.

"Yeah!" Speedy yelled. "They ruined our party. But I want to make sure we can see them clean up so they can't do anything else."

Mr. Zermeño held up his hand. "Why don't I grab some trash bags and everyone can help clean up the yard. I think Coach Quinn has some phone calls to make to these boys' parents."

The team collected empty trash bags from Mr. Zermeño and headed outside to take care of the mess the Jupiters had made. With so many people helping, it wouldn't take them long to clean up the yard. Frank and Joe picked Silly String up off the grass, while Tommy Dawson (the tallest member of the team) hoisted Iola (the shortest) onto his shoulders so she could reach the loops of toilet paper high in one of the trees. Speedy went back inside and grabbed a plate of cookies that everyone munched on as they worked.

"I'm going to take this bag inside and get another," Frank said when the trash bag he and Joe were sharing was stuffed with toilet paper and Silly String. "I'll be right back."

On his way to the kitchen for another trash bag, Frank passed Conor Hound and the other Jupiters. They were still sitting on the couch, waiting for Mr. Hound, who had agreed to take all three boys home. Coach Quinn was talking to them in her most disappointed voice. Frank actually felt kind of bad for them. If he knew anything about the coach of the Jupiters, Coach Riley, the joke would not be worth the extra minutes of running that the team would have to do at their next practice!

The player closest to Frank gave him a glare. "You'll be sorry," he said under his breath.

Well, maybe Frank didn't feel *that* bad for them. With his head turned to look at Conor and the others, Frank didn't notice Mimi lying on her stomach in his path until he'd tripped over her. She and the other younger kids were still spread out all over the living room floor, playing with the toys from Mimi's new backpack. The toys had invaded every surface, from the carpet to the coffee table.

"Hey!" Mimi squealed.

"Sorry!" Frank replied. He lifted his foot off her coloring book, which he'd accidentally stepped on. "I didn't see you."

Mrs. Morton poked her head around the corner. "Mimi, what did I say about getting in the way? Frank's the fourth person who's tripped over you tonight. How about you kids move into one of the bedrooms?"

"Mom!" Mimi protested. "Do we have to?"

While Mimi argued with her mother, Frank went into the kitchen to drop off his full garbage bag and pick up an empty one.

When he returned to the living room, Mimi and the younger kids were packing up her toys to move into one of the bedrooms, and Conor Hound's father had arrived. He'd already sent Conor and the other two players outside and was apologizing to Coach Quinn.

"I'm going to have a long talk with him tonight," he said.

"Smile!"

Frank was suddenly blinded by the flash of Chet's camera. He hadn't seen his friend approach, and now he couldn't see anything at all! He blinked to try to clear the bright dots from his vision.

"Hey, sorry!" Chet said. "I didn't mean to surprise you."

"Oh, that's okay," Frank said. "Can you help me back outside, though? I don't think I can make it on my own!"

Chet laughed and took Frank's arm. "Sure."

"Excuse me!" Mimi said.

The boys moved aside to let her pass. She had two stuffed animals cradled in her arms and more nearly spilling out of her partially unzipped backpack. She led the other younger brothers and sisters to one of the bedrooms so that no one else would trip over them.

Frank and Chet joined the rest of the Bandits outside, and soon they had finished cleaning the Zermeños' yard. Coach Quinn told them how proud she was of their teamwork as they came back inside the house and took the pieces of cake that Mrs. Zermeño had waiting for them. Then they all gathered together so that Chet could snap a team photo. After thanking the Zermeños for the party, everyone said good-bye and headed home.

PLAYBOOK PUZZLER

The next afternoon was their first official practice of the new season. The team was brimming with excitement as they gathered in the dugout at the Little League field. Frank took a deep breath, inhaling the smell of fresh grass and leather. As far as he was concerned, baseball season was the best time of the year.

Coach Quinn stood up in front of the team, her ever-present clipboard held in the crook of her arm, and everyone quieted down to listen to her instructions.

"I'm afraid I have some bad news, team," she said.

Frank exchanged a worried look with his brother.

"Remember the new playbook I showed you last night?" the coach said. "It's gone missing."

The team gasped.

"It went missing sometime during the party," Coach Quinn said. "Did any of you accidentally take it home with you?"

Frank looked at his teammates, but everyone was shaking their heads.

Coach Quinn sighed. She looked disappointed. "Well, I want you to check when you get home just in case, okay? That playbook is very important."

Frank swallowed. As far as he knew, he'd been the last one to look at the playbook.

"Okay, everyone," Coach Quinn said. "Time to get to work! Please break into pairs and do some catching and throwing."

Frank ran up to the coach as everyone else took the field to start practicing.

"Hey, Coach," he said. "I'm really sorry about the playbook."

"Thank you, Frank," she said.

"I put it on the coffee table in the living room when I was finished looking through it," Frank said. "Do you know if anyone else looked at it after I did?"

She shook her head. "I'm not sure. All I know is it was gone by the time I was ready to leave the Zermeños'. Don't worry, though. I'm sure it'll turn up."

Frank nodded and went to join Joe on the field. They began to toss a ball back and forth, listening to Coach Quinn's instructions about the best form to use as she weaved among the players, checking their progress.

When Coach Quinn was out of earshot, Joe said quietly to Frank, "I bet the playbook was stolen."

Frank shook his head. "Someone probably just took it by mistake."

"Oh, really?" Joe said. "What about what you told me that Jupiter said to you? 'You'll be sorry'? What better way to get back at us for getting them in trouble than by stealing our playbook?"

Frank thought about that. The boys' father, Fenton Hardy, was a private investigator, and he'd taught them how to look at the world through a PI's eyes. Frank thought back to the party and realized that the Jupiters players had been seated on the couch right next to the coffee table where he'd left the playbook. It would have been easy for one of them to swipe it when no one was looking, and Joe was right about one thing. It *would* be the perfect revenge.

"I guess it is possible," he said.

"Yes!" Joe said. "A new case for us to solve!"

Like their father, the boys had discovered they had a knack for solving mysteries. They'd already cracked several cases in Bayport and were always on the lookout for another. Frank wasn't convinced that this was a real mystery yet, but he decided to humor his brother just in case.

After practice was over, they returned home. But instead of going inside the house, they went to the woods out back where their father had built them a hidden tree house. They used it as their secret base of operations for all their investigations. Unless you knew what to look for, the tree house was perfectly hidden. Frank checked both ways to make sure no one was coming and then grabbed the rope they'd concealed behind a tree. When he gave it a tug, a rope ladder dropped down from the hidden tree house above. They climbed it quickly.

"Okay," Frank said once they were inside the tree house. He opened up the notebook where they kept track of clues for their investigations. "Let's start with the Five *W*s."

The Five *W*s was something else their father had taught them about investigations. Finding them was the key to solving any mystery. Frank took out his notebook and wrote them down.

"We don't know the *who*," Joe said, "but the *what* is the Bandits' playbook."

"*When* is sometime between when I looked at it after the team meeting and when Coach Quinn got ready to leave and noticed it was missing," Frank said. As he spoke, he filled in the answers in the notebook in his neat, straight handwriting. That was one reason he always took control of writing down the clues. Joe couldn't even read his own handwriting half the time.

"We should talk to everyone else who was at the party and see if anyone looked at it after you did," Joe pointed out. Frank made a note of it on the right side of the page, next to the Five *W*s.

Who was the last person at the party to see the playbook?

"The *where* is the Zermeños' living room," Joe said, "and the *who* and *why* are what we have to figure out!"

Chapter 5

A FURRY FRIEND

The boys joined the rest of the team on the field the next day for practice. Coach Quinn started the day off by asking them all a question.

"Did everyone check their things for the play-book yesterday?" she said.

The team nodded.

"Did anyone find it?" she asked.

Frank figured someone would say they had. It was a more likely explanation than the playbook having been stolen. But to his surprise, everyone shook their heads.

"I knew it!" Joe whispered. "It *was* stolen!"

"I guess you're right," Frank whispered back.

"That thief better watch out!" Joe said. "The Hardy brothers are on the case!"

The team took their positions to practice—which meant Frank behind home plate to catch and Joe at second base—so Frank didn't have a chance to talk to his brother about the playbook again until they were packing up their things to head home.

"Who do you think might have taken it?" Frank asked as he stuffed his mitt into his bag.

"That's easy!" Joe said. "We're still missing a *why*, right? That will lead us to our *who*! The thief has to be a person who had a *reason* to do it."

"A motive," Frank said. He and his brother started to walk across the park toward their house. "Either the thief wanted our playbook for themselves—"

"Or they just didn't want us to have it, " Joe said. "Neither motive fits for anyone on the Bandits."

"But *both* fit for the Jupiters players," Frank

pointed out. "Stealing our playbook is a great way to get back at us for getting them into trouble."

"Plus," Joe added, "it would give their team an advantage to know about all the special training ideas and plays that Coach Quinn put together."

"You're right," Frank said. "The Jupiters had the perfect motive."

Joe looked over at another team practicing at one of the other baseball diamonds at the park. "Hey, is that the Jupiters?"

Frank followed his brother's gaze. "Yeah, I think it is."

"Let's go over there," Joe said. "Maybe we'll discover something!"

Frank followed his brother to the field where the other team was practicing. Sure enough, it was the Jupiters. Frank would recognize Conor Hound anywhere, since he towered almost a foot above all the other kids on the team. Frank and Joe crept toward the dugout as the team practiced catching and throwing the way the Bandits had done the day before. As long as they stayed low to the ground, the team wouldn't be able to spot them over the roof of the dugout, which stuck up several feet out of the ground.

"Well, now what?" Frank whispered once they were crouched behind the dugout.

Joe shrugged. "We wait? Maybe when they come back here to pick up their stuff after practice, they'll talk about stealing the playbook."

"Maybe," Frank said. "What would really be good is if we could get into the dugout and see if the playbook is in there. If one of them stole it, they probably would have brought it here with them."

"Yeah, but how do we get in there without anyone noticing?" Joe asked.

"Uh, I'm still working on that part of the plan," Frank replied.

Joe sighed. "Well, let me know when you figure it out."

They watched the Jupiters practicing for a couple of minutes, Frank racking his brain for a plan. Suddenly there was a commotion in the far corner of the field. Frank shielded his eyes from the sun with one

hand as he tried to see what was going on. Two players were running toward the back of the field and
shouting, and in the distance Frank spotted Wilmer
Mack. Mr. Mack often brought his dog, Lucy, out
to the ball field for her daily walk, and Lucy loved
playing fetch more than anything.

"Hey, look!" Joe said, pointing. "It's Lucy! She
has their ball!"

Sure enough, there was Lucy with a baseball in
her mouth. The two Jupiters players who had been
tossing it back and forth were running after her,
trying to get their ball back. But Lucy just thought
it was part of the game. She dodged away from
them, leading them on a chase across the field.
Slowly, more and more Jupiters players went to help
until finally the whole team, Coach Riley, and Mr.
Mack were chasing Lucy, who was having the time
of her life.

"Now's our chance!" Joe cried, jumping to his
feet and rushing into the dugout.

"Joe!" Frank said. "Get back here!"

But Joe was already looking through the dugout

for the bright-red playbook. First he went through the coach's papers, which were stacked on the edge of the bench. Then he grabbed Conor Hound's backpack—which had his last name monogrammed on it in big letters—and began to look through that, too.

"They're going to catch you!" Frank warned.

"No way," Joe replied. "It will take them forever to catch Lucy. But if you come down here and help me, we'll be done twice as fast!"

Frank looked nervously out at the field. The team was still chasing Lucy, and they were now entirely off the field and halfway to the concessions stand. Someone could come back any second, but for now, the Jupiters were completely distracted.

"Oh man," Frank said, looking back and forth between his brother in the dugout and the Jupiters chasing the dog. "Fine! I'm coming!"

Frank jumped down into the dugout with Joe and started looking through the backpacks and gym bags the team had left scattered around. He felt a little bad about it, but he reassured himself that he wasn't hurting anything. Plus, the Jupiters had started it by vandalizing Speedy's yard and stealing the playbook in the first place.

"See anything?" Joe asked.

Frank shook his head. "Just equipment, clothes, and homework."

"Same here," Joe said.

Frank looked back over the field. The team had finally caught Lucy, and Mr. Mack was getting the ball back from her.

"We've got to go," Frank said. "They'll be headed back soon."

"Okay," Joe said. "There's nothing here anyway. Let's go!"

The two boys climbed out of the dugout and began to run back toward their house, in the opposite direction, just as the Jupiters started to return to the field to resume their practice.

"Maybe the Jupiters players weren't the ones who took the playbook after all," Frank said.

"Just because we didn't find the playbook doesn't mean they don't have it," Joe pointed out. "If it wasn't them, then who was it?"

Chapter

6

PHOTOGRAPHIC EVIDENCE

Frank and Joe returned home and had dinner with their parents and Aunt Trudy. Frank had trouble concentrating on his mother's story about what had happened at her job that day and Aunt Trudy's story about the book she was reading, because he couldn't stop thinking about the missing playbook. The Jupiters were the only people at Speedy's house that night who had any motive to steal it. Plus, they had been alone in the living room with the book more than anyone else, which gave them plenty of time to swipe it. He thought about it as they ate dessert, as they cleaned the table, and as he started to wash the dishes (it was his turn). If the Jupiters had stolen the playbook, wouldn't they have wanted to show it to their teammates and brag about what they'd done? Frank thought so. In that case, he and Joe should have found it in the dugout.

"Frank?" Mrs. Hardy called, shaking him from his thoughts.

"Yeah, Mom?" he said.

She held the phone out to him. "It's for you."

He wiped his hands dry on a dish towel and took the phone. "Hello?"

"Hey, Frank!" It was Chet on the other end of the line. "Do you and Joe want to come over and play video games tonight? My parents said it's okay."

Chet! Frank suddenly remembered that Chet had been snapping photos throughout the party. Maybe somewhere in his pictures he'd captured a clue as to who had taken the playbook.

Frank turned to his mother, who was drying the dishes he'd washed.

"Hey, Mom, is it okay if we go over to Chet's for a little while tonight?" he asked.

Mrs. Hardy gave him a look.

"Once I'm done with the dishes, of course," he added with an extra-sweet smile.

"I don't know, Frank . . . ," she said.

"Please, Mom!" Frank pleaded. He *had* to see those photos. Chet might have even photographed the theft itself!

"Is your homework done?" Mrs. Hardy asked.

Frank nodded. "Totally done. My chores, too."

Mrs. Hardy thought for a moment. Frank crossed his fingers and, for good measure, tried to cross his toes as well.

"All right," she finally said. "Just be home by eight, okay? It's a school night."

"I will," Frank promised. "Thanks, Mom!"

"Finish the dishes first!" Mrs. Hardy pointed to the sink.

Frank nodded and got back to scrubbing.

A few minutes later Frank and Joe walked over to the Mortons' house. On the way, Frank told Joe about his theory that there might be clues hidden in Chet's photographs from the party.

"Thank goodness for Chet's new hobby!" Joe said, and Frank laughed.

When they arrived, Chet answered the door and invited them into the house.

"I just got this new race-car game, Ultimate Driver," Chet told them as they went into the living room. "It's so cool. You're going to love it!"

"Not yet, Chet!" Iola said. She and Mimi were sitting on the carpet in front of the television, watching an animated movie about a horse. "Mom said you have to let us finish our movie before you can play."

"Yeah, sorry about that," Chet said to Frank and Joe. "They got here first, so we have to wait."

"That's okay," Frank said. "We were actually wondering if we could look at your pictures from the party."

"Sure!" Chet said. "I think they turned out pretty well. They're on my dad's computer. Follow me."

Chet led them upstairs, to a spare bedroom that Mr. Morton used as his home office. Chet sat down in front of the computer and jiggled the mouse to wake it up while Frank and Joe pulled up chairs. Chet opened up a folder, and a file with dozens and dozens of pictures in it came up. Frank exchanged a look with his brother. Going through Chet's pictures to look for clues was going to take a lot longer than he'd thought!

Chet started to click through the pictures. They started at the beginning of the evening, when everyone was in the Zermeños' backyard, eating and playing games. Joe asked Chet if he could skip ahead.

"What are you looking for?" Chet asked.

"Well, we want to see if there are any clues about who took the playbook Coach Quinn showed us that night," Frank said.

"Someone stole it?" Chet asked.

Of course, Frank realized. Chet wasn't on the team, so he didn't know that the playbook had gone missing. Frank explained to him that the playbook had disappeared at some point during the party.

"So you two are on the case, huh?" Chet asked.

Joe grinned. "Of course we are!"

"Well, let's see if I can help," Chet said. He clicked quickly through the pictures until he came to one of Coach Quinn standing in front of the team in the Zermeños' living room, holding the playbook in her hands. "I took this during the team meeting. This was the first time you saw the playbook, right?"

Frank nodded. "Yeah. Keep going, Chet."

Chet clicked slowly through the pictures. There were a couple more of the team meeting, then one of Ezra Moore and Tommy Dawson high-fiving.

In the background, Frank was looking through the playbook. In the next picture, Speedy was laughing with first baseman Jason Prime. Frank had disappeared from the background, and the playbook was sitting on the coffee table where he'd left it.

"Well, it looks like it wasn't *you* who stole it, Frank," Joe said.

Frank punched him in the arm while Chet laughed.

After that, the pictures moved outside. There were at least a dozen showing members of the team working together to clean up the Zermeños' yard.

"You can skip these," Joe said. "Did you take any more in the living room?"

"Sure did," Chet replied. He clicked forward until the pictures moved from the Zermeños' dark yard to their bright living room. There was one of several parents in the kitchen, smiling and waving at the camera. Then there was a picture of Frank looking shocked. Frank remembered he was holding a trash bag at that moment. He hadn't seen Chet there, and the flash of the camera had temporarily blinded him. Joe laughed at the goofy expression on Frank's face in the picture, but Frank studied the photo with sharp eyes.

"There!" Frank said. In the bottom corner of the picture was a splotch of red on top of the coffee table. It was a little fuzzy, but Joe had a feeling he knew what that red splotch was.

Joe put his face close to the computer and squinted at the picture. "Yeah, that's definitely the playbook."

Frank frowned and crossed his arms over his chest.

"What's wrong?" Chet asked.

Frank sighed. "The Jupiters didn't steal the play-book."

BANDIT BETRAYAL

"What?" Joe said. "How do you know?"

"Because the Jupiters were gone by that point," Frank said. "When I came out of the kitchen with the empty trash bag, Conor Hound's dad had already arrived and sent them outside to wait for him."

"Are you sure?" Joe said. "Maybe Mr. Hound didn't arrive until later."

"I'm positive," Frank said. "That was the only time I went inside while we were cleaning the yard."

"You know what, I think you're right," Joe said. "When you went inside, I went over to help Speedy instead. I remember she and I were trying to get some toilet paper out of a tree with a rake when we saw the Jupiters getting into Mr. Hound's car."

"But the playbook was still on the coffee table right where I left it," Frank said, pointing to the red splotch in the picture. "The Jupiters couldn't have stolen it. Which means . . ."

"What?" Chet asked.

"It means it was one of *us* who stole it," Frank said slowly. "One of the Bandits."

"Oh man," Joe said, leaning back in his chair with a frown.

All three boys just looked at one another for a moment. Frank's stomach suddenly ached. He didn't *want* to solve this mystery anymore. Not if the thief was someone on his own team.

"Keep going, Chet," Joe finally said. "Maybe there are more clues to find."

Chet continued to click through the pictures, but neither the coffee table nor the playbook could be seen in any of them. Until he reached the last picture. It was the photograph he'd taken of most of the team at the end of the night. They all had their arms around one another, big grins on their faces.

On the coffee table in front of them, the play-book was nowhere in sight.

Frank and Joe decided to forget about the case for the rest of the night. It made them both too sad to imagine that one of the Bandits had stolen the playbook. Instead they played video games with Chet and tried not to think about it.

By the next morning, though, Frank was once again determined to find out who was behind the playbook's disappearance. The thief might be someone he liked, but he still had to get to the bottom of the mystery. He owed that to Coach Quinn and the rest of the team. Joe told him at breakfast that he'd woken up feeling the same way.

"The thing I don't get," Joe said over pancakes at the kitchen table, "is why any of the Bandits would have a *motive* to steal the playbook. It hurts the team, and whoever they are, they're on the team! It doesn't make any sense."

Frank had been thinking about the same thing. Why would a Bandit want to hurt the Bandits?

"I don't understand it either," he said. "Do you remember anyone acting strangely that night?"

Joe shrugged. "Not really. Oh! Except Tommy Dawson. He was in a really bad mood, remember?"

"Oh yeah!" Frank said. "He was upset about not getting to pitch."

"Right!" Joe exclaimed. "He was supposed to pitch in Speedy's place because of her hurt wrist. But when Speedy got better, Coach Quinn told him she was going to start Speedy instead."

"He was pretty angry about that," Frank remembered. "Maybe angry enough to want to get revenge on Coach Quinn . . ."

"By stealing the playbook she made," Joe finished. "Would Tommy have had a chance to do it? The team was together most of the night. When would he have taken it?"

Frank thought back to the night of the party. The playbook went missing sometime between when the Jupiters left and when Chet took the group photo at the end of the night. For most of that time, the team was outside cleaning up the Zermeños' yard, but kids did come and go from the yard the whole time they were out there.

"He might have had a chance," Frank said, "if he went inside while the rest of us were in the yard. The younger kids were playing in Speedy's bedroom by then, and most of the parents were in the kitchen. There wouldn't have been anyone in the living room to see him swipe the playbook."

"But did he go inside while we were in the yard?" Joe asked.

"Only one way to find out," Frank said. "Hurry and finish your breakfast quick. We've got to stop by the Mortons' before school!"

Joe wolfed down the rest of his pancakes, and he and Frank left for school. They usually walked anyway, so today they made a detour to Chet's house on the way.

"Hey, guys!" Chet said when he answered the door. He looked happy to see them but puzzled. "What are you doing here?"

"Can we look at those pictures again, Chet?" Frank asked.

Chet checked his watch. "I think we've got time if we hurry! What are you looking for?"

The three boys ran upstairs to Mr. Morton's office while Frank explained their new theory. Chet fired up the computer and found the pictures he'd taken of the team outside cleaning, the same ones they had skipped the night before. They went through them slowly, scouring the pictures for clues, their faces just inches from the computer screen.

"There!" Joe said.

The photograph was of Speedy holding an armful of toilet paper. In the background was the front door of her house. It was partially open, spilling light across the lawn. Tommy Dawson was stepping inside.

"He *did* go inside while we were working," Frank said, "which means he would have had the chance to take the playbook."

Joe nodded. "I guess it's time to talk to Tommy. Let's get to school!"

Chapter 8

PITCH WARS

"You ready?" Frank asked his brother when they spotted Tommy Dawson near the gym after school. They'd been keeping an eye on Tommy's gym locker ever since the bell rang. They had baseball practice right after school, so they knew Tommy would eventually go to his locker to pick up his gym bag.

"I'm ready," Joe said. "Let's do this."

Joe approached Tommy as he reached his locker

and started to spin the combination lock. Frank waited farther down the hall. Tommy looked up when Joe approached.

"Hi, Joe," he said. "How's it going?"

"Pretty good," Joe replied. Then he launched into the conversation he and Frank had rehearsed. "I just wanted to say, I'm really sorry you're not going to be pitching in the first game."

"Thanks," Tommy said, putting his math book down and grabbing some stuff from his locker. Joe moved to the other side of the locker, so that Tommy would have to turn his back to his open locker to face him.

"The truth is," Joe continued, "I think you're a better pitcher than Speedy any day."

"You and me both," Tommy said, getting annoyed. "It's so unfair! Coach Quinn told me *I* was going to get to pitch in the first game. Just because Speedy got better faster than anyone expected shouldn't change anything."

With Tommy's back turned to him while he was complaining to Joe, Frank crept toward Tommy's open locker. If Tommy had stolen the playbook, the odds were high that this was where he was keeping it. A private place with a lock on it.

"Yeah, that's really uncool," Joe said.

Tommy crossed his arms over his chest. "I bet Coach Quinn just wants to put Speedy in because she's a girl like the coach. I can't believe a *girl* is getting to pitch over me."

Frank rolled his eyes behind Tommy's back. Speedy was the best pitcher in the league. It had nothing to do with her being a girl. Frank quietly inched Tommy's locker door open enough that he could peer inside.

"This whole thing makes me so mad," Joe said. "It almost . . ."

"What?" Tommy asked.

"Well . . . ," Joe said. Frank had never realized just how good an actor his brother was. He really seemed upset on Tommy's behalf. "It almost makes me want to get back at the coach somehow, you know?"

Tommy's locker was a mess of papers, books, broken pencils, and dirty clothes. Frank didn't see the playbook, but it could easily be buried under all the junk crammed inside. Frank reached inside and began to move things around, moving slowly and carefully so as not to make any noise.

Meanwhile, Tommy didn't take the bait Joe had laid out for him. Instead he just shrugged and said, "It's not *that* big a deal. It just made me mad, you know?"

"Yeah, I get it," Joe said, "but are you sure you want to let Coach Quinn off the hook that easy?"

Tommy looked at Joe with sudden suspicion in his face. "What are you trying to say?" he asked.

Uh-oh. Frank knew he had to move fast. He moved a couple of Tommy's textbooks and looked underneath a dirty (and kind of smelly) T-shirt. He still didn't see the playbook, but that didn't mean it wasn't still buried in there somewhere. . . .

Joe said, "I'm not saying anything, Tommy."

"Are you trying to ask me if *I'm* the one who took the playbook?" Tommy asked. "To get back at Coach Quinn for letting Speedy pitch instead of me?"

"No!" Joe said. "I just—"

Tommy started to turn back to his locker. Frank saw the movement from the corner of his eye as he rooted around for the playbook, but it was too late. Tommy was going to catch him in the act.

"No way, man!" Joe exclaimed, grabbing Tommy's shoulders so he couldn't turn. "I would never think that, Tommy!"

Frank snatched his hand back from the locker

and leaned against the wall as he tried to catch his breath. He didn't know how real private investigators like his dad handled all this excitement!

Joe found him there a minute later after saying good-bye to Tommy.

"Did you find anything?" Joe asked.

Frank shook his head. "The playbook might have been in there, if he buried it at the bottom of the mess, but I didn't see it."

"I don't know about this, Frank," Joe said. "Tommy seemed really upset at me for thinking he'd taken the playbook. It didn't seem like an act."

"I know what you mean," Frank said, "but right now, we don't have any other suspects. Tommy had the opportunity to take it *and* a motive. He's the only one we can think of with any reason to want the playbook to disappear."

Joe frowned. "We've got to be missing something."

"I agree," Frank said. "But what?"

Chapter 9

HIDING SPOT

Frank and Joe decided to take a break from the case for the rest of the day. They were a little stumped and didn't know what to do next. Their dad always said that sometimes the best thing you could do was to think about something else for a while instead. After baseball practice—which Chet attended to get some pictures of the team in action—Frank asked him if they could hang out that afternoon.

"That would be great!" Chet said. "Want to come to my house? We can play Ultimate Driver again."

"Sounds good!" Frank and Joe said.

The three boys went over to Chet's house, and Frank called his mom to let her know where they were before they sat in the living room to play Chet's new racing game. Chet wasn't very good at sports like Frank and Joe, but he was awesome at video games. In fact, he was crushing them. His red car zoomed ahead of their green and blue ones, tearing around corners and flying over obstacles. At one point Iola came into the living room to watch.

"Come on, Frank!" she cheered. She always rooted for the underdog, and Frank's green car was at the back of the pack. "You can do it!"

"Hey!" Joe complained. "What about me?"

"Or me?" Chet asked. "I'm your brother!"

"Sorry," Iola replied. "Frank needs my cheers the most!"

"Ha-ha, thanks a lot," Frank said, but he secretly appreciated her support.

Unfortunately, Iola's cheers couldn't make Frank's

car move faster. Chet's car raced across the finish line first, and Frank was a distant third.

"Yes!" Chet shouted, pumping his fist in the air. Frank and Joe both gave him high fives.

Mrs. Morton appeared in the doorway. "Anyone want a snack?"

"Yes, please!" everyone said.

Mrs. Morton brought them a plate of apple slices with peanut butter. Mimi, with her pink backpack on, followed her into the living room.

"Chet, Iola," Mrs. Morton said. "Can you keep an eye on your sister for a minute? Jeanine from next door is having some kind of baking emergency and needs my help."

"Sure thing, Mom," Chet said.

After they'd eaten the apple slices, Joe challenged Chet and Frank to an Ultimate Driver rematch. Iola decided she wanted to play too and chose a yellow car to drive. They offered to let Mimi join the game, but she wasn't interested. Instead she unzipped her backpack and turned it upside down. A small avalanche of toys, crayons, and coloring books came tumbling out of it. Mimi selected an orange crayon and began to color in a picture of a giraffe.

"I'm going to get you this time, Chet!" Joe said as the race began. Chet's red car zoomed into the lead, but halfway down the course, Joe took a tight turn on the racetrack that cut his lead in half. Joe was almost as good at video games as Chet was.

"Keep dreaming, Joe!" Chet teased. "You'll never beat me!"

Out of nowhere, Iola's yellow car passed everyone else.

"Take that, boys!" she said, laughing.

Meanwhile, Frank accidentally crashed his car into a tree and fell farther behind. "Oh man!" he said.

Joe, Chet, and Iola were locked in a fierce battle for first place. Frank was working hard to catch up, but he knew it was hopeless. The finish line approached, and Joe's car inched ahead. Frank could see that Joe was crossing his fingers, which made it hard for him to hold the controller.

"Come on!" Joe said, urging his car forward.

Joe's car raced across the finish line first, and he jumped up and did a victory dance. Frank and Chet groaned good-naturedly, while Iola laughed and threw a couch cushion at him.

"Good race, guys," Chet said.

"Thanks," Joe said. "Want to go again?"

"Yeah!" Iola said.

"I'm going to take a break this round," Frank said.

"What, are you chicken?" Chet teased.

Frank made a squawking sound, and everyone laughed. While they cued up the game, he sat next to Mimi on the carpet.

"Hey, Mimi," he said. "Have you started preschool yet?" He remembered that was why her parents had bought her the backpack in the first place. She'd been so excited to start school when he'd last seen her, at the Bandits' party.

Mimi nodded without looking up from her picture. "Yeah, I started this week."

The others had begun another race and were whooping, hollering, and teasing one another. Frank picked up a green crayon.

"Do you mind?" he asked, pointing to the tree the giraffe was eating from. It hadn't been colored in yet.

"Go ahead," Mimi said.

"So, are you liking school?" Frank asked as he started to color in the leaves of the tree.

"Yeah, it's pretty cool," Mimi said.

"Are you learning to read?" Frank asked.

"Not yet," she said, "but we're learning letters, and we play lots of games, and there's recess and snack, and my best friend Jill is in my class, and my teacher is really nice. . . ."

Mimi talked nonstop about school after that. She could give Speedy a run for her money when it came to words spoken per minute. Together she and Frank colored in the giraffe picture and another one that featured two lions drinking from a watering hole. Chet, Iola, and Joe were playing another round of Ultimate Driver when Mrs. Morton came home from the baking emergency next door.

"Mimi," she said, "it's almost time for ballet. Better start getting ready."

"Okay, Mom," Mimi said. She scooped up all the toys and crayons and shoved them into her backpack. Then she ran out of the room to get ready for her dance class.

Frank moved back to where the others sat in front of the television. They'd had enough of Ultimate Driver and were putting in a different video game. But something was bugging Frank as he tried to beat the evil lizard king in the new game. Something he couldn't put into words yet, something that had struck him when he'd seen Mimi picking up her toys earlier. . . .

"Earth to Frank!" Iola said. "Are you going to pick up that power crystal or just stare at it?"

Then, all of a sudden, it became clear. Frank dropped his controller.

"I know what happened to the playbook!" he exclaimed.

Can you solve the mystery? How did Frank figure out what happened?

And, most importantly, who took the Bandits' play-book?

THE HARDY BOYS—and
→ YOU! ←

CAN YOU SOLVE THE MYSTERY OF THE MISSING PLAYBOOK?

Grab a piece of paper and write your answers down. Or just turn the page to find out!

1. Frank and Joe came up with a list of suspects. Can you think of more? List your suspects.

2. Write down the way you think the brand-new Bayport Bandits' playbook disappeared.

3. Which clues helped you to solve this mystery? Write them down.

PLAY BALL!

"Wait, what?" Joe said, glancing at Frank as he dropped his controller too.

"I figured out who stole the playbook!" Frank repeated. "Well, not *stole* it exactly."

Iola paused the game. "Well? Tell us!"

"I can do better than that," Frank declared. "I can show you."

Frank ran up the stairs to the second floor of the Mortons' home, followed by Joe, Chet, and Iola.

He turned left at the top of the stairs and headed to Mimi's room, which had a pink and purple sign on the door bearing her name. Frank knocked, and Mimi—dressed in her ballet uniform—opened the door.

She cocked her head at them. "What do you want?"

"Can we come in for a second?" Frank asked.

She let them inside and Chet asked, "What's going on, Frank?"

"Mimi, do you remember what you were doing the night of the Bandits' party?" Frank asked.

The little girl nodded. "Me and the other little kids were playing."

"Where?" Frank asked.

"In the living room, mostly."

"On the floor," Frank said. "Just like you were downstairs just now, right?"

"Yeah," she said. "So?"

"So a lot of people tripped over you, didn't they?" he asked.

"I guess," she said. "*You* stepped on my coloring book."

"I sure did," Frank agreed. He turned to the

others. "It was right after I came inside to get a new trash bag. I tripped over Mimi, went into the kitchen for the bag, and when I came out, the Jupiters were gone. That's when you took that picture of me, Chet."

"The one that showed that the playbook was still on the coffee table," Chet said.

"Right," Frank said. "The playbook was still on the coffee table after I got the new trash bag, but sometime between then and the end of the night, it disappeared. Mimi, do you remember what happened after I tripped over you and stepped on your book?"

Mimi nodded. "Mom made me and the other kids move to Speedy's bedroom so we wouldn't be in the way."

"What did you have to do in order to move?" Frank asked.

"Put my toys and stuff into my backpack."

"Oh!" Joe said. "I get it! Mimi, where do you keep all your toys?"

Mimi pointed to a small chest underneath her window.

"Do you mind if we look in it?" Joe asked.

She shrugged. "I guess not."

Joe opened the chest, and he and Frank rifled through it. There were dozens of stuffed animals, building blocks, action figures, and coloring books. And then, near the bottom, sandwiched between two coloring books, was a bright-red notebook with PLAYBOOK written on the front in block letters. Frank held it up in triumph.

"You found it!" Iola shrieked. She gave Frank and Joe high fives.

Chet laughed. "So *Mimi* stole the playbook?"

Frank smiled. "Not on purpose. Mimi can't read

yet. When her mom told her to pack her things and move to the bedroom, she accidentally grabbed it along with her coloring books."

"Oops!" Mimi said, giggling. "Sorry!"

Everyone laughed, and Chet gave his youngest sister a hug and assured her it was okay.

"Case closed!" Frank said.

Well, not quite. First they had to return the playbook. At baseball practice the next day, Coach Quinn started with her usual pep talk and instructions. Before she could finish, though, Frank raised his hand.

"Yes, Frank?" the coach asked.

"I was just wondering," Frank said, reaching into his bag, "if you were still looking for this?"

He showed her the playbook, and the team erupted into applause. Coach Quinn took the playbook back with a big smile.

"Good work, Frank!" she said happily. "You found it!"

"With Joe and Chet's help," Frank said.

"Well, in that case," Coach Quinn said, "I think

I'll have to treat my whole team—and the team's official photographer—to ice cream cones after practice!"

The team cheered, and Chet snapped a picture.

"Okay, everyone!" Coach Quinn clapped her hands. "Let's get to work!"

As everyone was moving to their positions to start practice, Frank and Joe caught up to Tommy Dawson.

"Hey, Tommy," Joe said. "I'm sorry I accused you of stealing the playbook with no proof."

Tommy sighed. "It's okay. I was being a real jerk about Speedy. I would have suspected me too."

"So, friends?" Joe asked.

Tommy grinned. "You bet."

After baseball practice, Frank and Joe went into the woods behind their house and climbed the rope ladder to their hidden tree house. Joe took out their notebook and a pen.

"I'm glad Tommy wasn't the person who took it," Frank said.

"Me too," said Joe. "And I am really happy we cracked this case!"

Don't miss the next

HARDY BOYS
Clue Book:
#3 WATER-SKI WIPEOUT

As the tour bus pulled up outside the lodge, Frank and Joe Hardy could see the lake in the distance. Bucks Mountain, the tallest mountain near their hometown, Bayport, was right behind it.

"You think we could hike all the way to the top?" Frank asked, turning to his younger brother.

"It's probably too steep," eight-year-old Joe replied. "Besides, don't you want to spend all day out on the boat? That's why I brought the skis."

Nine-year-old Frank looked at the luggage rack above them. His brother's new water skis were tied together on the roof with a bright blue strap. Last summer Joe had started water-skiing at camp. In just a few weeks, he'd gotten really good. He even tried to ski for a few seconds on just one ski—even though he usually ended up in the water! Joe was so excited about it, this year their parents had bought him his very own set of skis for his birthday. And it was just in time for the third and fourth graders' school trip to Lake Poketoe. This would be the very first time he used them.

"You'll have to teach me," Frank said. "I doubt I'll be as good as you."

Ellie Freeman's head popped up over the seat in front of them. She was wearing her Bayport Bandits T-shirt. She was on their baseball team, and she liked wearing the uniform even when she didn't have to. "You promised to teach me, too," she said, looking at Joe. "I want to learn how to do a flip!"

Joe laughed. "Like the professionals do? That's really hard. I don't think I'm going to be able to do that for a while!"

The bus came to a stop, and Ellie hopped out of her seat. She grabbed her duffel bag from the rack above. "I guess I can try. . . . Are you guys going to the barbecue tonight?"

"You bet," Joe said. "Mr. Morton promised he'd make his famous smoked ribs." Mr. Morton, their good friend Chet's dad, was one of the parents who had come along on the school trip. Suzie Klein's mother had also come, but as far as Joe knew, she didn't make the ribs as good as Mr. Morton's.

Joe reached for the water skis, but they came down with a clatter as he tried to take them down.

"Ow! Watch it, Hardys."

Frank and Joe turned around to see Adam Ackerman in the seat behind them. Adam was in Frank's grade at school. He was sitting with his friend Paul. Adam was on the aisle, and he kept rubbing the side of his head.

"You hit me with those stupid skis!" Adam complained. He stood up, yanking his bag down with a huff. "You're going to pay for that, Hardy."

He pushed past them, nearly knocking Joe over.

Paul followed close behind. He was a short boy with a large, round face. He always wore his brown baseball cap turned to the side. "Watch your back, Hardy," he grumbled.

"Just ignore them," Frank said. "It's not worth it."

But Joe's cheeks were hot. He felt like everyone on the bus was staring at him. "Let's go," he said, careful not to knock anyone else with the skis.

Adam was one of the biggest bullies at Bayport Elementary. He was taller than most of the kids and was always saying mean things or pushing people around. Frank and Joe tried to stay away from him, but even they had trouble with him sometimes.

The Hardys followed Ellie out of the bus, looking at the lake in front of them. A few kids had dropped their bags on the rocky beach. They crowded around Mrs. Jones, one of the parents who had come on the trip. She gave them directions as to which cabins were theirs. Frank and Joe found out they'd be staying in the lodge itself.

Just hearing the birds chirping put Joe in a better mood. The afternoon sun was out and the water looked cool and refreshing. A few yards away, a boat was zipping across the lake. A girl was in an inner tube behind it, screaming as it pulled her along.

"Frank and Joe Hardy! What a pleasant surprise!" Mrs. Rodriguez called out from the lodge. She'd been Joe's second-grade teacher, and she was one of the adults who'd come on the other bus. It was funny to see her in plaid shorts and a pink T-shirt. Joe hadn't ever seen her outside the classroom!

"This is the best!" Joe called out. "Glad we caught the last few hours of sunshine."

"It's good to have you here, just in case. . . . You never know what might happen!" Mrs. Rodriguez smiled. Just a few months ago Joe and Frank had helped her find a ring that she'd lost. She'd thought someone at school had stolen it, but the boys figured out that wasn't true. They eventually found it in one of her desk drawers.

It wasn't the first case they'd solved, though. Frank and Joe were known around Bayport for solving mysteries. Once it was a lost video game, and another time it was a missing playbook. Their father, Fenton Hardy, was a private detective. He'd taught them everything they knew about investigating. He showed them how to interview suspects and search a crime scene for clues.

Joe dragged his water skis behind him. He was happy the path to the lodge wasn't that long—the bag was getting heavy! They followed the rest of their group into the lodge. There was a huge living room with couches. A few deer heads were on the wall above the fireplace.

"Whoa," Frank whispered. "That's kind of creepy."

"It's like a real log cabin," Joe said. He pointed to the ceiling, where you could see all the wood beams. It reminded him of the toys he and Frank played with when they were really little.

Frank looked out the back windows, toward the lake. There were a few smaller cabins there, hidden in the trees. He saw Adam and Paul go into one of them with their bags. The sign over the door said PINECONE CABIN.

Just then Chet Morton came down the hallway. "Did you guys pick your bunks yet?" he asked. "You should come check out our room! We left you a top and bottom bunk!"

They followed him down the hall, to a room with two sets of bunk beds. Mr. Morton was sitting on one. He pulled a jar of red stuff from his bag. "My secret rib sauce!" He smiled. "I'll need this for tonight."

Frank and Joe laughed. "I call dibs on the top bunk!" Joe declared. He looked around, realizing there wasn't a good place to leave his skis. "Where should I put these?" he asked. "They take up the whole room."

"There's a shed out back," Chet said. "Here, I'll show you."

As Chet ran out the door, his dad called after him. "You can go explore, but make sure you're back in an hour. Dinner will be served!"

Chet showed Frank and Joe the storage shed behind the lodge. There were a dozen other cabins around it. Joe put his skis inside, next to a pile of life vests. Then the boys followed Chet down to the dock.

"Wow, there are kayaks!" Frank said.

"And we can use that tomorrow morning," Chet added, pointing to a white speedboat tied to the dock. "Joe, remember, you promised me you'd teach me to water ski!"

"He promised you . . . and me . . . and Ellie . . . and half the school," Frank laughed. "It's going to be a long day."

Joe smiled as they walked back to the lodge. A crowd had gathered on the deck. Mr. Morton, Mrs. Rodriguez, and some of the other adults were cooking dinner. Some kids were sitting at the round tables, drinking lemonade. Ellie and a few of her friends were tossing a softball back and forth on the grass below.

As the sun set, Joe could almost picture what it would be like tomorrow. All his friends would be out on the boat. He'd teach them how to do different tricks on his water skis. Maybe they'd even go tubing after.

"Who's ready to eat?" Mr. Morton called out. A bunch of kids cheered.

Joe, Frank, and Chet all cheered along with them. One thing was certain: this was going to be the best school trip yet.

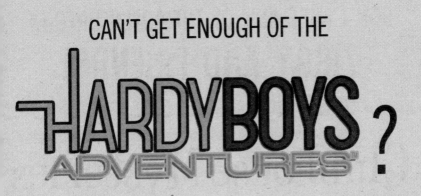

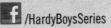

Join Zeus and his friends
as they set off on the
adventure of a lifetime.

Now Available:

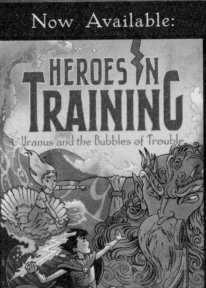

HEROES IN
TRAINING
Uranus and the Bubbles of Trouble

Joan Holub & Suzanne Williams

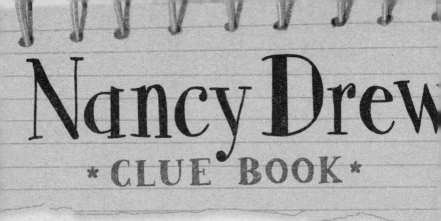

Nancy Drew
★ CLUE BOOK ★